WALT DISNEY'S CLASSIC

Based on Walt Disney's
full-length animated classic

Adapted by Jan Carr

SCHOLASTIC INC.
New York Toronto London Auckland Sydney

ISBN 0-590-41171-3

12 11 10 9 8 7 6 5 4 3 2 1   7 8 9/8 0 1 2/9

Printed in the U.S.A.   11

First Scholastic printing, October 1987

Cinderella

1

Once upon a time, in a faraway land, there was a tiny kingdom. There, in a stately chateau, lived a gentleman. He had been widowed, and so he lived alone with his little daughter, Cinderella. Cinderella was a beautiful child. She had long silken hair, bright clear eyes, and pretty smiling lips. Everyone loved the little girl. She was as kind and as good as she was beautiful.

Cinderella's father was devoted to her. He gave Cinderella every luxury and comfort. But still he felt that the little girl needed a mother's care, and so he married again. His second wife, Lady Tremaine, had two daughters just Cinderella's age. One was named Anastasia, the other, Drizella.

All went well in the household for a time. One day, however, very suddenly, the good man died. Cinderella was then left alone with her stepmother and stepsisters.

By this time, Cinderella had become a beautiful, charming young woman, and her stepmother was bitterly jealous of her. Lady Tremaine was actually quite cold and cruel. Now that Cinderella's father was gone, she made Cinderella do all the work in the house. Her own two daughters did none at all. Cinderella had to scrub the floors. She had to wash the clothes. She had to sweep the hearth. No longer treated like a daughter, Cinderella became a servant in her own house. Yet, through it all, she remained gentle and kind. Each dawn, when she awoke, she tried to remember the happy things she had dreamed during the night. And each morning she found herself hoping that, someday, her dreams would come true.

2

One bright morning, the sun streamed through the curtains of Cinderella's tiny attic room. Cinderella lay in bed, still asleep. From outside, right through the window, some birds flew in. They fluttered around Cinderella's head, chirping gaily. Some were robins. Some were bluebirds. All were Cinderella's friends. One little bird hovered near Cinderella's ear. Another tugged at her braid.

"Cinderella," they chirped. "Cinderella, wake up."

Cinderella opened her eyes. She was still a little drowsy.

"Yes, I know. It is a lovely morning," she said. She sat up on the edge of her bed. "But it was a lovely dream, too."

"Dream?" the birds chirped. "What kind of dream?"

Cinderella smiled. "Oh, I can't tell," she said. "If you tell a wish, it won't come true."

Cinderella loved to sing. Often, she started the morning with a song. That morning, she sang a song about dreams and wishes. In her sweet, lilting voice, she explained to her friends:

"A dream is a wish your heart makes,
When you're fast asleep,
In dreams you will lose your heartaches,
Whatever you wish for, you keep!
Have faith in your dreams and some day,
Your rainbow will come smiling through.
No matter how your heart is grieving,
If you keep on believing,
The dream that you wish will come true!"

There was a lot of work to do that morning, just as there was every morning. Cinderella bustled about, getting ready. Her animal friends helped. The robins and bluebirds fluttered about, making Cinderella's bed and helping her bathe. There were also many little mice who lived in Cinderella's room. They gathered her clothes for the day, and brushed them clean.

Just as Cinderella finished her song, a mouse scrambled in from under the door. He scampered onto her dresser and chattered excitedly. He was trying to tell Cinderella something.

"Wait a minute. Wait a minute. One at a time,

please," said Cinderella. "Now, Jaq, what's all the fuss about?"

Jaq was a funny little mouse. He wore a coat and cap.

"New mouse!" he shouted. He jumped up and down. "New mouse in a house!"

"Oh, a visitor," said Cinderella. She opened a little box she had. It was full of tiny, mouse-sized clothes. She had sewn them for her friends.

"No, no, no!" said the other mouse.

"Gotta get him out," shouted Jaq. "In a trap-trap. Gotta get him out!"

"In the trap?" said Cinderella. "Well, why didn't you say so?"

She hurried out the door and ran down the stairway. Jaq and the other mice ran after her, close behind.

3

Down the stairs on a landing, there was, indeed, a trap. It was a big cagelike trap. Inside was a chubby little mouse. He was crouched against a corner, trembling and very frightened.

"Why, the poor little thing's scared to death," said Cinderella.

Cinderella let Jaq into the cage. Maybe he could explain things to the little mouse. Jaq walked across the cage. He walked slowly, carefully.

"Flinderella," he said, in his funny way of talking. "Zuk, zuk. Flinderella."

The scared mouse didn't understand at all what Jaq was saying. Why was Jaq coming toward him? Maybe Jaq wanted to hurt him. The mouse made a fist, jumped up, and took a swing at Jaq, trying to hit him.

"No, now, look-a, little guy," said Jaq. "Nutta worry 'bout. We like-a you."

The little mouse blinked at him.

"Flinderella like-a you, too," said Jaq. "She's-a nice."

The little mouse looked up at Cinderella. Cinderella smiled down. Why, it was true. She did look nice. The little mouse smiled slowly back.

"Atsa better," said Jaq. "Come on." He put his arm around his new friend and led him out of the cage.

Cinderella had brought down some of her tiny, mouse-sized clothes. In her hand she had a little sweater, a tiny hat, and two small shoes. She pulled the sweater over the mouse's head. He slipped, and tumbled on his rear. This little mouse wasn't used to wearing clothes.

"Hmm. It *is* a little snug," said Cinderella. "But it'll have to do."

The next thing he needed was a name.

"A name. . . . A name. . . ." Cinderella thought. "I've got it!" she said. "Octavius! But for short," she added, "we'll call you Gus."

Jaq jumped up and down, excited. "Like it, Gus?" he asked. "Like it? Like it?"

Gus nodded his head and laughed.

"Now, I've got to hurry," said Cinderella. She still had all her morning chores to do. "See that he keeps out of trouble, Jaq," she said. She started down the stairs. "Oh," she remembered. She called back to Jaq. "And don't forget to warn him about the cat."

The cat! If Gus was going to live in the house, he'd certainly better know about Lucifer. Lucifer was Lady Tremaine's pet, and all the mice were afraid of him.

"Mean!" said Jaq. "Sneaky!"

Gus had never seen a cat. "Cat cat?" he asked.

"Big as a house!" Jaq warned. "Meow!" He jumped at Gus.

Gus fell backward off the step.

"Jump-a-choo!" said Jaq. "Bite-a-choo!"

Gus listened wide-eyed. He was scared.

4

On the second floor were three very large, very beautiful bedrooms. Lady Tremaine slept in one, and Cinderella's two stepsisters took the others. Lucifer, the cat, slept on the second floor, too. He had his own special bed in Lady Tremaine's room. It was soft and cushioned.

In the morning, Cinderella's first job was to feed Lucifer. She tiptoed quietly down the hall and opened Lady Tremaine's door.

"Here, kitty," she called softly. "Here, kitty-kitty-kitty-kitty."

Lucifer did not want to get up. He yawned and rolled over, away from Cinderella.

Cinderella did not like Lucifer any more than the mice did.

"Lucifer," she called again.

He yawned. He stretched. He yawned some more. Then Lucifer padded lazily out the door and followed Cinderella down the stairs.

"I'm sorry if Your Highness objects to an early

breakfast," said Cinderella. "It's certainly not my idea to feed you first."

Lucifer waited outside the kitchen while Cinderella went in. Bruno the dog was in there. Lucifer and Bruno were sworn enemies.

Though Bruno was asleep on his rug, he was kicking his feet around and growling fiercely.

"Bruno!" Cinderella called.

Bruno woke up with a start.

"Were you dreaming again?" asked Cinderella. She took the dog's head in her hands. "Were you chasing Lucifer?"

Bruno nodded.

"Did you catch him this time?" asked Cinderella.

Bruno nodded and smiled, remembering.

"Oh, Bruno," said Cinderella. "That's bad."

With Cinderella in the room, Lucifer was safe. He walked up to Bruno and sat beside him. When Cinderella wasn't looking, he flicked his tail in Bruno's face.

Cinderella was busy with the breakfast dishes.

"You should think of Lucifer's good points," she told Bruno. She tried to think of something nice to say about Lucifer. She couldn't think of a thing.

"Hmmm," she said. "Well, there must be something nice about him."

Lucifer looked at Bruno slyly. He slipped his

paw under Bruno's rug. He bared his claw and scratched the dog. Hard.

Bruno jumped up and growled. Lucifer just meowed, as innocently as he could.

"Bruno!" said Cinderella. "I know it isn't easy, but at least we should *try* to get along together."

She set Lucifer's bowl of milk down in front of him.

"That goes for you, too, Your Majesty," she said.

There were still many other animals to feed that morning. Cinderella opened the kitchen door and stepped into the barnyard.

"Everybody up!" she called. "Breakfast! Breakfast!"

All the barnyard animals came running.

5

B ack in the kitchen, behind a small hole in the baseboards, the mice could hear Cinderella calling for breakfast. Of course, they wanted their breakfast, too. If they could get out to the barnyard, Cinderella would give them some. But to get to the barnyard they needed to go through the kitchen. And to go through the kitchen, they needed to get past the cat. For there was Lucifer, sitting right by the doorway, drinking his milk. What would they do? Jaq had a plan.

While the others watched from the mousehole, Jaq snuck out into the kitchen. Lucifer didn't see him. He was leaning on one paw and dabbing the other into his bowl of milk. Jaq crept up beside the cat and gave Lucifer's paw a swift kick. Pow! Lucifer fell face-down into his milk. When he tried to raise his head, Jaq splashed at him again.

That did it! Lucifer would get that mouse! Jaq tore off and Lucifer chased after him. The other mice peeked out their hole. Now was their chance.

One by one they inched their way out, along the kitchen wall and toward the door. Jaq was safe. He had found a hiding place. Would Lucifer notice the rest of them?

They made it! The last of the mice ran out the kitchen door and into the bright barnyard.

"Oh, there you are," said Cinderella. "I was wondering." She tossed the mice handfuls of the corn she had been feeding the others.

Most of the mice were good at this. They gathered the corn up quickly and scurried back. Gus, the new mouse, was not as quick.

"Poor little Gus," said Cinderella. She put some more kernels on the ground just for him. "Here," she said. "Help yourself."

Gus stacked his kernels as best he could and ran after the others. He still had to get his breakfast back through the kitchen, and past Lucifer.

Gus probably would have made it. But when he was running in, he came upon another kernel. It was on the floor. Someone else had dropped it.

Gus stopped to pick it up. He set his stack down on top of it. The new stack was awfully high. Gus tried to lift it, but he couldn't. He dropped the whole thing, and kernels scattered all over the floor. He scrambled to gather them up, but it was too late. There he was, face to face with Lucifer.

Gus ran, but Lucifer caught him by the tail. Jaq had tried to warn him about cats. "Jump-a-choo!"

Jaq had said. "Bite-a-choo!" Oh, if only he had listened.

Luckily, Jaq was watching from his hiding place behind a broom. He knew just what to do. Bam! He knocked the broom over, right onto Lucifer's head. Gus jumped out from under Lucifer's claw and escaped. He ran up the leg of the kitchen table and climbed into a teacup.

Lucifer was right behind. He had Gus now. Before Gus could escape again, he clapped the teacup over. Gus was trapped underneath. All Lucifer had to do was lift up that teacup and grab him.

RRRINNNG!

Lucifer was startled by the sound of a bell. It was the bell that Lady Tremaine and the stepsisters used to call Cinderella.

RRRINNNG!

It sounded again. It was loud and insistent.

"Cinderella!" a voice called out.

"I'm coming," said Cinderella. She hurried back through the door, across the room, and over to the kitchen table.

6

Lady Tremaine and the stepsisters wanted breakfast, and they wanted it right away. Cinderella bustled around the kitchen, getting the trays ready. She didn't see poor little Gus, trapped under the teacup. She didn't wonder why Lucifer was lurking around. She grabbed the other two teacups and set them upside down on their saucers. Lucifer looked at the cups, confused. Which one was Gus under?

The bell rang again. Cinderella gathered up the trays and started up the stairs. Lucifer was not about to lose Gus again. He followed behind, close on Cinderella's heels.

Cinderella knocked at the first door and entered.

"Good morning, Drizella," she said cheerfully. "Sleep well?"

"Hmmmmph," Drizella answered. "As if you cared."

She sniffed at her breakfast.

"Take that ironing," she ordered. "Have it back in one hour. You hear? One hour."

"Yes, Drizella," said Cinderella.

Cinderella picked up the laundry and continued down the hall. Lucifer followed her into the second bedroom.

"Good morning, Anastasia," said Cinderella. She set down her stepsister's breakfast tray.

"Well, it's about time," said Anastasia.

Cinderella started out of the room.

"Don't forget the mending," Anastasia barked after her. "And don't be all day getting it done, either."

"Yes, Anastasia," said Cinderella.

Cinderella delivered the last breakfast tray to her stepmother. Lady Tremaine had even more jobs to add to Cinderella's long list.

"Pick up the laundry," she said, "and then get on with all your other chores."

As Cinderella was about to leave the room, a terrible scream pierced the air. It was Anastasia. She had just lifted up her teacup and had found poor little Gus.

"Mother! Mother!" she shouted.

Gus scampered out of the cup, off the bed and out the door. Lucifer was waiting for him in the hall. He had his claws poised and open. Gus ran right into them. Anastasia ran into her mother's room.

"A big ugly mouse!" she cried. "Under my tea-cup! Cinderella did it! She put it there!"

Cinderella hurried out into the hall to look for Lucifer. There he was, right outside Anastasia's room. She knew right away what had happened.

"All right," she said to Lucifer. "Come on. Let him go."

She lifted the cat up. There was Gus, underneath his foot.

"Oh, Lucifer," said Cinderella.

Gus scrambled away, into a nearby mousehole. Once again that day, he was saved.

"Cinderella!" Lady Tremaine called from her bedroom. She was angry. If Cinderella had nothing better to do than play nasty tricks, then she would just have to think of more jobs for her.

"Now let me see," she said. "There's the large carpet in the main hall — clean it. And the windows upstairs and down — wash them. Oh yes, and the tapestries and draperies. . . ."

"But I just finished those," said Cinderella.

"Do them again!" shouted her stepmother. She was hardly finished. "Don't forget the garden," she went on. "Then scrub the terrace, sweep the halls and stairs, clean the chimneys, and, of course, there's the mending and the sewing and the laundry."

Poor Cinderella! How would she ever finish?

Lady Tremaine looked down at Lucifer. Sweet

little Lucifer. Innocent little Lucifer. Lucifer could do no wrong. She smiled at her pet and stroked his ears.

"Oh, yes," she said. She thought of one last job for Cinderella to do. She smiled at her cat.

"See that Lucifer gets his bath," she said.

7

That morning, the Tremaine household was not the only one in bad temper. Across the kingdom, in the castle, the King himself was angry — royally angry. He was angry at his son, the Prince. He wanted the Prince to get married. He wanted the Prince to have children. He called the Duke into his chambers to talk to him about it.

"My son has been avoiding responsibility long enough!" the King shouted. He pounded his fist on his desk. "It's high time he married and settled down."

"Of course, Your Majesty," said the Duke, "but we must be patient."

"I am patient!" shouted the King. He picked an ink bottle up off his desk. He threw it against the wall. "But I'm not getting any younger, you know," he said. "I want to see my grandchildren before I go."

"I understand, Sire," said the Duke.

"No you don't," shouted the King. He started

to sniffle. "You don't know what it means to see your only child grow further away." He laid his head against the Duke's chest and began to cry. "I'm lonely in this desolate old palace," he said.

"Now, now, Your Majesty," said the Duke. "Perhaps if we just left the Prince alone. . . ."

"Let him alone!" the King shouted. He was angry again. "With his silly romantic ideas?"

The King was not about to sit around and wait for the Prince to fall in love. Who could know when *that* might happen? The King had ideas of his own. His idea was to hold a ball for the Prince. They would invite all the eligible young women in the kingdom.

"But, but Your Majesty," said the Duke.

"The boy's coming home today, isn't he?" said the King.

"Yes. . . . Yes, Sire," said the Duke.

"Well, what could be more natural than a ball to celebrate his return?" said the King. "If all the eligible young women in the kingdom just happened to be there, he's bound to show interest in one of them, isn't he?"

The Duke could hardly argue. "Yes, Sire," he said.

The King ordered the Duke to arrange the ball.

"Soft lights," he said. "Romantic music. All the trimmings."

"Very well, Sire," said the Duke. It would be

a big job, but he'd have to do it. "When do you want the ball?" he asked.

"Tonight," said the King.

"Tonight?" stuttered the Duke. He was stunned. There wasn't time.

"Tonight!" ordered the King. "It can't fail. And make sure every eligible young woman is there!"

8

Cinderella was in the front hall, scrubbing the floor, when she heard a knock on the door.

"Open in the name of the King!" someone called.

Cinderella opened the door. It was a messenger.

"An urgent message from His Imperial Majesty," he said. He handed Cinderella a letter.

"From the King!" Cinderella's mice friends gathered around. "What's it say?"

Cinderella curtsied to the messenger and shut the door.

"I don't know," she said.

Down the hall, in the piano room, Lady Tremaine and the stepsisters were having their music lesson. Drizella was singing at the top of her lungs. Anastasia was accompanying her on the flute. Unfortunately, neither of them could carry a tune. The sound of the music was awful. Even Lucifer had fled the room.

Cinderella examined the letter. She had strict

instructions never to interrupt the music lesson.

"But the messenger says it's urgent," she said. She knocked at the music room door.

Lady Tremaine was angry when she saw Cinderella.

"I've warned you never to interrupt us," she said.

"But this just arrived," said Cinderella. "From the palace."

"From the palace!" said Drizella. She snatched the letter.

"Let me have it," said Anastasia. She snatched it back.

"I'll read it," said Lady Tremaine. She stepped in and took the letter herself.

"Well," she announced. "There's to be a ball."

"A ball!" cried the stepsisters.

Lady Tremaine continued. "It's in honor of His Highness the Prince. By Royal Command," she said, "every eligible young woman is to attend."

"Why, that's us!" said Drizella.

"I'm so eligible," said Anastasia.

Cinderella's heart soared. She stepped into the room.

"Why, that means I can go, too," she said.

Drizella looked at her and started to laugh.

"Ha!" she said. "*Her* dancing with the Prince? Ha! Ha!"

"Well, why not?" said Cinderella. She would not

be laughed at. "I'm still a member of the family. And besides, it says, by Royal Command, every eligible young woman is to attend."

Lady Tremaine looked down at the letter.

"Yes, so it does," she said. There was no getting around it. Cinderella was right.

"Well," said Lady Tremaine. "I see no reason why you can't go." She shrugged her shoulders. "That is, if you get all your work done."

"Oh, I will. I promise," said Cinderella.

"And," said the stepmother, "if you can find something suitable to wear."

"Oh, thank you, Stepmother," said Cinderella. "I'm sure I can." She hurried out of the room to get started. If she was going to go to the ball, she had a lot to do.

Anastasia looked at Drizella. Drizella looked at Anastasia. Had they really heard their mother right? Had their mother actually said that Cinderella could go to the ball?

"Mother!" said Drizella. "Do you realize what you said?"

Lady Tremaine smiled slyly. She knew *exactly* what she'd said.

"Of course," she sneered. "I said 'if.' "

"Oh," said Drizella. It all came clear.

"If," smiled Drizella.

Lady Tremaine nodded and laughed a vicious laugh.

9

High up in her attic room, packed away in a dusty trunk, Cinderella did have a dress.

"Maybe it would be just the thing to wear to the ball," she said.

She opened the trunk and pulled the dress out. The mice and birds gathered around to see.

"Isn't it lovely?" she said to her friends. She held the dress high. "It was my mother's."

None of the animals knew quite what to say. Maybe the dress had once been beautiful. Maybe a long time ago. But now. . . . Well, it was hardly a dress to wear to a ball. One of the mice stepped forward carefully.

"But-a," she said. "But-a dress old."

"Maybe it is a little old-fashioned," said Cinderella, "but I'll fix that."

Cinderella took a book from her sewing basket and paged through it.

"There ought to be some good ideas in here,"

she said. "Aha!" She found just the one. "This one."

Cinderella pointed to the picture.

"I'll have to shorten the sleeves," she said. "I'll need a sash and a ruffle and something for the collar. And then I'll. . . ."

"Cinderella!"

Someone was calling her from downstairs.

"Oh, now what do they want?" said Cinderella. She touched her dress longingly. She had so many ideas.

"Cinderella! Cinderella!"

"Oh, well," said Cinderella. "I guess my dress will just have to wait."

"Cinderella!"

"All right. All right. I'm coming," she called.

Jaq and Gus watched sadly as she ran back down the stairs.

"Poor Cinderelly," said Jaq. "Every time she finds a minute, that's the time when they begin it. Cinderelly! Cinderelly!"

As all the other mice gathered around, Jaq began his angry song.

> "Cinderelly . . . Cinderelly . . .
> Night and day it's Cinderelly
> Make the fire, fix the breakfast,
> Wash the dishes, do the mopping,
> And the sweeping and the dusting,

They always keep her hopping;
She go around in circles,
Till she very dizzy . . .
Still they holler . . . keep-a-busy,
Cinderelly!"

"You know what?" said Jaq, when he finished. "Cinderelly not go to the ball."

"What?" said another mouse.

"You'll see," said Jaq. "They'll fix her. Work. Work. Work. She'll never get her dress done."

One of the little girl mice was sitting in front of Cinderella's book. She looked at the open page.

"Hey!" she said. She had an idea. "*We* can do it! We can help our Cinderelly!"

10

Downstairs, just as Jaq had predicted, the stepsisters had lots of work for Cinderella to do.

"Here, Cinderella," said Drizella. "Take my dress."

"Mend my buttonholes!" said Anastasia.

"And press my skirt!" said Drizella.

"And Cinderella!" said Lady Tremaine. "When you're through, and before you begin your regular chores, I have a few other things for you to do."

"Very well," said Cinderella.

She didn't know that right upstairs her little friends were already hard at work. As the animals scurried around, getting the dress ready, they sang a new song:

"We can do it, we can do it,
We can help our Cinderelly!
We can make the dress so pretty,
There's nothing to it, really!

We'll tie a sash around it,
Put a ribbon through it;
When dancing at the ball,
She'll be more beautiful than all. . . .
In the lovely dress we'll make
For Cinderelly. . . .
Hurry, hurry, hurry, hurry,
Gonna help our Cinderelly,
Got no time to dilly dally,
Gotta get-a goin'!"

All of the little animals were busy, some cutting, some sewing.

"We need more trimming!" said a mouse.

Jaq and Gus knew just what to do. They scurried out the door. They'd find something pretty, something beautiful, to add to the dress.

As it happened, just then, Drizella and Anastasia were going through their closets. They were throwing out all the things they didn't like.

"Why look at this sash," said Anastasia. "I wouldn't be seen dead in it." She threw the sash to the ground.

"Well, look at these beads," said Drizella. "They're trash. I'm sick of looking at them." She kicked the beads across the floor.

A sash! Beads! Just the things! Jaq and Gus scooted across the floor and grabbed them up.

They dragged the booty to their mousehole and back upstairs.

In the little attic room, quite a miracle had already taken place. The mice and birds had fixed the faded, plain dress. They had added pretty bows and sashes. Now, it was a beautiful gown. It was fit for any ball, even one so grand as the Prince's.

Cinderella was still downstairs, working on the mending. She sat by the window and gazed longingly out. She could see the castle just beyond. Carriages were already pulling up, bringing eligible maidens to meet the Prince. Now she would never get to go.

Cinderella had no idea what her animal friends had accomplished.

11

From the window, Cinderella saw a carriage pull up in front of her own house. That would be the carriage for her stepmother and stepsisters. She went to tell Lady Tremaine.

"Oh," said her stepmother, looking at her. "Why, Cinderella, you're not ready, child."

"I'm not going," said Cinderella.

"Not going?" said Lady Tremaine. "What a shame." She looked at her daughters and smiled. "Of course, there will be other times."

"Good-night," said Cinderella, simply.

Cinderella climbed the steps back to her room. Her face was long. She couldn't help it. She was thinking of how wonderful it would've been to go to the ball.

The room was dark when she entered. Cinderella sighed and gazed out the moonlit window. Suddenly, the room lit up all around her. There were her friends, the birds and the mice. The birds flew up and opened the doors to a screen. There, behind the screen, was her beautiful party dress.

"Surprise!" yelled her friends.

Cinderella looked at the dress in shock.

"Why, I never. . . . How can I ever. . . . Why, thank you so much," she cried.

In a flash, Cinderella was dressed, and racing down the stairs.

"Please! Wait for me!" she shouted.

Anastasia and Drizella were shocked to see that Cinderella had indeed gotten ready on time. Where had she gotten that dress? They were not at all pleased to see that Cinderella looked so very beautiful.

"Cinderella!" said Anastasia.

"Mother! She can't go!" cried Drizella.

Lady Tremaine smiled. "Well, we did make a bargain. Didn't we, Cinderella?" she said. She walked menacingly toward the girl. "And I never go back on my word."

Drizella and Anastasia stared at their mother. Had she gone crazy? Was she really going to let Cinderella go to the ball?

A nasty smile played on Lady Tremaine's lips. She touched the beads on Cinderella's neck.

"How very clever," she sneered. "These beads. . . ."

Drizella looked. She recognized the beads immediately. Why, those were *hers*, the ones she had just thrown away.

"Why, you little thief," she cried. "Give them here." She grabbed at the beads and tore them right from Cinderella's throat.

"And that's my sash!" cried Anastasia. She pulled at the dress and ripped the sash away.

Lady Tremaine did not stop her daughters. The girls continued to tear at Cinderella.

"Sneak!" they yelled. "Thief!"

They pulled at her and ripped at her dress until her beautiful ballgown was nothing more than rags.

"Girls!" cried Lady Tremaine. "That's enough! Hurry along now. Both of you!"

She and her daughters turned and walked haughtily to the carriage that waited for them.

Cinderella ran crying into the garden.

"It's no use at all," she sobbed. "There's nothing left to believe in."

But, as she was crying, a strange thing happened. Magic lights began to flicker in the night, and an odd-looking woman appeared. The woman was old and round. She wore a funny cape that fell over her shoulders and covered her head. The woman took Cinderella's head in her lap and caressed her hair.

"Come now, dry those tears," she said brightly. "You can't go to the ball looking like that."

12

Cinderella looked up at the strange woman, and then down at her own torn clothes.

"Oh, but I'm not going to the ball," she said.

"Of course you are," said the woman. "But we'll have to hurry, because even miracles take a little time."

"Miracles?" said Cinderella.

"Mmmhmm," said the woman. She looked around. "Now what in the world did I do with my magic wand?" she mumbled to herself. "I was sure I. . . ."

"Magic wand?" said Cinderella.

"That's strange," said the woman. "I always. . . ."

Cinderella looked at her. Who was this woman talking about miracles? Of course! "Why, you must be . . ." she started.

"That's right," said the woman. "I'm your Fairy Godmother."

Then, with a simple wave of her hand, she produced a magic wand.

"Now let me see," she said. "I'd say the first thing you need is a pumpkin."

"A pumpkin?" asked Cinderella.

"Mmmhmm," said the Fairy Godmother.

And what happened after that truly was a miracle. Her Fairy Godmother did find a pumpkin. She waved her magic wand at it and said a little something. Then that pumpkin, that plain, ordinary garden pumpkin, turned right into a beautiful coach.

"Oh, it's beautiful," said Cinderella.

The Fairy Godmother had used some very special magic words: "*Salaga Doola Menchicka Boola Bibbidi Bobbidi Boo.*" She sang a song for Cinderella, to tell her how they worked.

"Salaga doola menchicka boola,
Bibbidi bobbidi boo. . . .
Put 'em together and what have you got. . . .
Bibbidi bobbidi boo.
Salaga doola menchicka boola . . .
Bibbidi bobbidi boo. . . .
It'll do magic, believe it or not,
Bibbidi bobbidi boo!
Now, salaga doola means
Menchicka booleroo,
But the thingamabob

44

That does the job
Is bibbidi bobbidi boo!
Salaga doola, menchicka boola,
Bibbidi bobbidi boo. . . .
Put 'em together and what have you got,
Bibbidi bobbidi, bibbidi bobbidi,
Bibbidi bobbidi boo!"

"Well," said the Fairy Godmother, when she finished her song. "With an elegant coach like that, we'll simply have to have mice."

"Mice?" asked Cinderella.

The Fairy Godmother gathered together four of Cinderella's little mice friends. Two of them were Jaq and Gus. She again gave a wave of her wand. Suddenly, the mice were transformed into four handsome white horses.

After that, she turned a common horse into a coachman. And finally, she turned faithful Bruno into the coach footman.

"Well, well, my dear," she said when she was through. "Hop into the coach. We can't waste time."

Cinderella looked down. She was still wearing her old dress, the one her stepsisters had torn to shreds.

"Good heavens, child!" said the Godmother. "You can't go in that!"

Quick as a flash, she turned Cinderella's dress

into a rich, flowing ballgown, more beautiful than Cinderella ever could have imagined.

"Did you ever see such a beautiful dress?" Cinderella exclaimed. She looked down at her feet. "And look! Glass slippers!" she cried. "Why, it's like a dream, a wonderful dream come true."

"Yes, my child," said her Godmother, "but I'm afraid that, like all dreams, this can't last forever. At the stroke of twelve, the spell will be broken." At midnight, she explained, all of the magic — the coach, the horses, the dress — would suddenly disappear.

"I understand," said Cinderella. "It's more than I ever hoped for."

Cinderella stepped into the coach. The horses were prancing in place, ready to take her to the ball.

"Have a good time," said the Fairy Godmother. "Now, off you go."

As her coach pulled off, Cinderella pinched herself. Maybe she was still dreaming. There she was, in an elegant coach. She had her own horses and coachman and footman. She was wearing a beautiful gown. But, best of all — and this Cinderella could hardly believe — she was on her way to the Prince's ball.

13

At the ball, things were not going at all as the King had planned. Many young women were there, but the Prince wasn't interested in any of them. Each girl stepped up to the Prince to be introduced. To each, the Prince bowed politely . . . then he turned his head and yawned.

The King was watching from above. "I can't understand it," he said. "There must be at least one who would make a suitable wife."

The next to be introduced were Anastasia and Drizella. They stepped up to the Prince as the court announcer read their names. This time, however, as he bowed, the Prince saw someone across the room. A beautiful someone, who stood at the entranceway. It was Cinderella.

Immediately, the Prince was taken with Cinderella's beauty. He rushed past the stepsisters and strode down the long, guard-lined hall. When he reached Cinderella, he took her hand in his. Then he brought it to his lips and kissed it.

The King, of course, was thrilled.

"Quick! The waltz!" he called to the orchestra leader.

At once, Cinderella and the Prince began to dance. As everyone watched in awe, they danced across the ballroom. Then the Prince waltzed Cinderella onto the balcony and down the steps to the palace garden.

"Well," said the King. "Now for a good night's sleep."

The King was sure that everything would now work out exactly as he planned. The boy was in love, wasn't he? All the Prince had to do now was propose. What could possibly go wrong? The King left the Duke in charge.

"See that they're not disturbed," he instructed. "And when the boy proposes, notify me immediately."

Out in the garden, Cinderella and the Prince continued their moonlit waltz. They both knew that something wonderful, something magical, had suddenly happened to them. Cinderella began to sing.

"So this is love,
So this is love,
So this is what makes life worthwhile. . . .
I'm all aglow, and now I know,

The key to heaven is mine.
My heart has wings,
And I can fly,
I'll touch every star in the sky.
So this is the miracle
That I've been dreaming of. . . .
So this is love!"

Indeed, it was a beautiful night. All around them, trees waved gently in the night breeze. Above them, shooting stars chased each other across the dark sky.

The Prince walked Cinderella up a bridge. It overlooked a shimmering pond. There, the Prince took Cinderella in his arms.

Just as they were about to kiss, chimes sounded. Clock chimes. Cinderella jumped away.

"Oh! Oh, my goodness!" she exclaimed.

"What's the matter?" asked the Prince.

"It's midnight," said Cinderella. She started to go.

"No, wait!" said the Prince. "You can't go now."

"I must," said Cinderella. "Oh, please — the Prince! I haven't met the Prince yet."

"The Prince?" said the Prince. "But didn't you know?"

Cinderella didn't hear him. She had already run off. She ran back up the stairs, through the ball-

room, and down the palace steps. On the steps, as she fled, one of her slippers fell from her foot. She would have stopped to pick it up, but there was no time. She ran on to the coach that waited below.

The Prince ran after her.

"Wait!" he called. "Please come back! How will I find you? Wait! Please wait!"

He didn't even know her name.

14

The Prince was not the only one chasing Cinderella. As Cinderella ran through the ballroom, she ran past the Duke. He looked up in surprise. Where was she running?

"Oh, I say," called the Duke. "Young lady! Wait!"

By the time he took off after her, she had already reached the palace steps. He had to stop her.

"Guards! Close the gates!" he shouted.

With the clock still striking the hour, Cinderella jumped into her coach. The coach bolted off. It sped through the gates before they closed.

"Follow that coach!" shouted the Duke.

At his command, the palace horsemen jumped on their steeds and galloped after Cinderella. They chased her coach through the gate and then down a winding hill. They were gaining. It seemed they might catch her.

At the last stroke of twelve, however, Cinderella's coach turned suddenly back into a pumpkin.

The swift, running horses changed, too, back into mice. The guards raced past. They trampled the pumpkin, never even realizing. Cinderella and the animals watched from the side of the road.

"I guess I forgot about everything," she said to her friends. "Even the time." She sighed, recalling her time at the ball. "But he was so handsome. I'm sure that even the Prince himself couldn't have been so wonderful."

Once again, Cinderella was dressed in tatters. She stood up to make her tired way home.

"Look!" said Jaq and Gus, staring at her feet. "Look! Your flipper, Cinderelly. Your flipper!"

There, on Cinderella's foot, was the other glass slipper. It had not changed back! The Fairy Godmother had left her one memento of her wonderful night. Cinderella took the slipper off and held it in her hand.

"Thank you," she said, looking up toward the heavens. "Thank you for everything."

15

Back at the castle, the Duke was in quite a pickle. Cinderella had escaped right from under his very nose. What in the world would he ever tell the King?

The Duke knocked timidly at the King's chamber door.

"Come in!" said the King. He smiled to see the Duke. This must mean good news, he thought, the news he had been waiting for.

"So, the Prince has proposed already," he said. "Tell me all about it. Who is she? Where does she live?"

The Duke did *try* to tell the King what had happened, but the King was very excited. He didn't hear a word the Duke said.

"We've got to discuss arrangements for the wedding," said the King. "Invitations, a national holiday, all that."

"But, Your Majesty," said the Duke.

The King pulled out a cigar and gave it to the Duke. "Got to practice passing these out," he said. He was already thinking of the many grandchildren he would have.

"Sire," said the Duke. There was no way around it. He would just have to blurt out the news. "Sire, the girl got away."

"She what?!?" The King's face turned red. He was not pleased at all. "You traitor!" he shouted. He drew out his sword. "Treason! Sabotage!"

"I tried to stop her," the Duke sputtered, "but she vanished into thin air."

"Likely story," thundered the King.

"It's true, Sire," said the Duke. "All we could find was this glass slipper."

The King came after the Duke with his sword.

"But, Sire," said the Duke. "He loves her. He's determined to marry her."

"What?" said the King. "What did you say?"

"The Prince swears he'll marry only the girl who fits this slipper," said the Duke.

The King grabbed the slipper from the Duke and kissed it.

"Aha! We've got him!" cried the King. If the Prince said he would marry the one who fit the slipper, all they had to do was find a girl to fit the shoe. Any girl.

"You'll try this shoe on every young woman in

my kingdom," said the King. "And if the shoe fits, bring her in."

"But, Sire," said the Duke, "this shoe may fit any number of girls."

"That's the Prince's problem," said the King. "He's given his word. We'll hold him to it."

16

Early the next morning, in the town square, the Duke posted an official proclamation. Everyone in town was abuzz, talking about it. The Prince was going to marry the girl who fit the slipper! When Lady Tremaine heard the news, she hurried home. She had plans for her two daughters. Big plans.

Drizella and Anastasia were still asleep.

"Get up this instant!" their mother ordered. "We haven't a moment to lose. The Duke will be here any minute."

"Huh? Why?" asked Anastasia.

"Huh? Who will?" asked Drizella.

"The Duke!" shouted Lady Tremaine. "He's hunting for that girl, the one who lost her slipper at the ball."

Cinderella stood at the door, with the breakfast trays. She heard every word.

"They say the Prince is madly in love with her," said Lady Tremaine.

Cinderella gasped. "The Prince!" she whispered. Is that who she'd been dancing with? She hadn't realized.

"Get dressed!" Lady Tremaine ordered her daughters. "If they find a girl who fits the slipper, then, by the King's command, that girl will be the Prince's bride."

"His bride!" whispered Cinderella.

Drizella and Anastasia jumped to obey their mother. No one knew who that girl was. That meant they had a chance at the Prince.

"Get my things together right away, Cinderella," said Drizella.

"Not until she irons my dress," said Anastasia.

But Cinderella was in a daze. The Prince's bride! She could hardly believe her ears. She dropped the clothes her stepsisters gave her and wandered dreamily out the door.

Lady Tremaine watched Cinderella suspiciously.

"Mother!" said Drizella. "Did you see what Cinderella did?"

"Are you just going to let her walk out?" asked Anastasia.

"Quiet!" ordered Lady Tremaine.

As Cinderella wandered up the stairs, Lady Tremaine followed her. She wasn't sure what Cinderella was up to, but she didn't like the look of it. Nothing was going to interfere with her plans for her daughters. Nothing. Cinderella reached the top of the stairs and walked into her room. Lady Tremaine closed the door behind her, turned the key, and locked her in.

Cinderella ran to the door.

"Let me out!" she cried. "Please! You can't do this! You just can't!"

Up in the rafters, looking down, Jaq and Gus had seen the whole thing.

"She can't lock up Cinderelly," said Gus. "She can't do it."

On the other side of the door, Lady Tremaine sneered. She dropped the key into her pocket and started back down the stairs.

"We gotta get that key, Gus-Gus," said Jaq. "We just gotta get that key!"

17

Downstairs Anastasia and Drizella scrambled around, getting ready. The Duke's coach pulled up to the door. Anastasia, at the window, was the first to see.

"Mother, he's here," she shouted. "Do I look all right?"

Lady Tremaine hurried to the door. She opened it wide.

"Announcing his Imperial Grace, the Grand Duke," said the footman.

Lady Tremaine bowed deeply.

"M'Lord," she said. "You honor our humble home."

"Quite," said the Duke. He entered the house. Behind him, the footman carried in the glass slipper. It lay upon a satin pillow.

"Why, that's my slipper!" said Drizella.

"Well, I like that," said Anastasia. "It's *my* slipper."

"Girls!" shouted Lady Tremaine.

The Duke unrolled his scroll and began to read the royal proclamation.

In all the excitement, no one noticed Jaq and Gus. The two little mice had snuck into the room and were crouching on the table. They peered over the edge, into Lady Tremaine's pocket. There was the key, all right. Now all they had to do was get it. Gus held Jaq's tail and lowered him slowly down.

The Duke finished reading the proclamation and dropped to a chair.

"Let us now proceed with the fitting," he said.

Anastasia was the first to try. When she had seated herself comfortably, the footman took her foot and tried on the shoe. It slipped right on!

"There!" said Anastasia. "It's exactly my size."

Actually, of course, it wasn't her size at all. The footman hadn't slipped it onto her foot, only over her big toe.

"Well, it may be a trifle snug today," said Anastasia. "You know how it is. Dancing all night."

The footman tried pushing the slipper. He tried pounding it. But Anastasia's foot was too big. The slipper just would not go on any farther.

"Young man," said Anastasia. "I don't think you're half trying."

By this time, Jaq was in Lady Tremaine's pocket. He had the key in his hand. He lifted it out. Gus hung over the edge of the table, reaching for it.

They almost had it. Suddenly, Lady Tremaine shifted in her seat. Jaq, Gus, and the key all went flying. The two mice landed on the key and slid across the room, to the hall.

"Come on, Gus," said Jaq. "Flurry up-a stairs."

They didn't have much time. They had to free Cinderella before the Duke left the house.

"Thissa way," said Jaq. "Up up up."

In the parlor, Anastasia was still trying to squeeze on the slipper. She pushed her foot harder into the footman's face.

"Enough of this!" said the Duke. "Let's try the next young lady."

Time was running out.

18

Cinderella was in her room, kneeling by her door and sobbing, when she heard a noise. Why, what was that? She peeked through the keyhole to see. There was Jaq! There was Gus! Gus had the key!

"Us-a tummin', Flinderelly," cried Jaq. "Us-a tummin'."

Unfortunately, Cinderella was not the only one to see the two little mice. Lucifer the cat saw them, too. From the shadows, he watched. He waited. Just as Gus was about to squeeze under Cinderella's door, Lucifer pounced. He clapped a bowl right over Gus. And also over the key!

"Let him go, Lucifer!" said Cinderella.

Lucifer was not about to let go of any mouse. He'd waited a long time for this moment. He smiled and pulled the bowl closer to him.

When Jaq saw what had happened, he spun around. This was no time for Lucifer to play cat and mouse! They had to get the key to Cinderella.

The little mouse ran right up to Lucifer. He grabbed the cat by the tail and bit down as hard as he could. Ya!

At the same time, the other mice peeked out from their mousehole. Lucifer was spoiling everything! Cinderella needed their help! The mice ran back into their hole and armed themselves with forks. They flew at Lucifer. Charge! With one swoop of his paw, Lucifer knocked them all back.

Lucifer laughed. This was easy. Or so he thought. Clank! A plate hit him on the head. It was Cinderella's bird friends, flying overhead. They had plates in their beaks. They dropped them like bombs on Lucifer's head. Lucifer cowered, but still he held his paw tightly over the bowl.

Bruno! Cinderella had an idea. "Get Bruno!" she yelled to the birds. "Get Bruno quick!"

Downstairs, in the parlor, the footman was still trying to fit the slipper on Drizella's foot.

"I'll do it myself," she said. She took the slipper out of his hands. "I'll *make* it fit."

Drizella squeezed her toe into one end, and her heel into the other. The rest of her foot arched up high in between.

"There!" said Drizella.

The slipper fit, but it was tight. Drizella's foot arched higher. The slipper flew right off.

"Madam," sighed the Duke. He had had enough of this household. He was ready to leave.

Just at that moment, Bruno raced through the barnyard. He bounded into the house and up the stairs. Where was that cat? Bruno hated Lucifer! He'd do anything to save Cinderella!

Growl! Bruno reached the top of the stairs. Lucifer backed up, away from the bowl, toward the wall. Bruno dove at him. The cat jumped up on the window ledge to escape, but Bruno leapt right at him. Lucifer fell out the tower window. He dropped down, straight down, to his death.

"Come on!" cried Jaq. He grabbed the key from under the bowl, and scurried under Cinderella's door.

19

Downstairs in the front hall, the Duke was preparing to leave.

"You are the only ladies of the household, I hope. I mean, I presume," he said.

"There's no one else, Your Grace," said Lady Tremaine.

"Good day," said the Duke. He would certainly be glad to get out of this house. He put on his hat and started out the door.

"Your Grace! Your Grace!" called a voice.

Lady Tremaine and her daughters looked up. There, on the landing of the stairway, stood Cinderella.

"Please wait," she said. She ran to the Duke. "May I try it on?"

"Pay no attention to her," said Lady Tremaine.

"It's only Cinderella," said Drizella.

"Our scullery maid," said Anastasia.

The Duke raised his monocle to his eye and looked at Cinderella. He broke into a smile.

"Madam," he said. He brushed Lady Tremaine aside. "My orders were — *every* young woman. Come, my child," he said to Cinderella. He led her over to a chair.

Curses! This was not at all what Lady Tremaine had planned. She looked slyly from side to side. She still had one last trick up her sleeve. The footman was running right by her. He held the slipper on the pillow, bringing it to Cinderella. Lady Tremaine stuck out her cane, just as he passed by. He tripped. The glass slipper flew off the satin pillow and crashed to the floor. It shattered in a thousand pieces.

"Oh, no!" cried the Duke. "This is terrible. The King! What will he say?"

Cinderella reached behind the chair.

"Perhaps I can help," she said.

"No, no," the Duke cried. "Nothing can help now."

"But you see," said Cinderella, "I have the other slipper."

It was true. There, in her hand, Cinderella held a glass slipper, just like the other. The Duke was so happy, he kissed it. Then he slipped it on Cinderella's foot.

It fit like a glove. Of course it did. It was Cinderella's all along. The Duke had found the girl, the one the Prince was looking for. Cinderella would be the Prince's bride!

20

Just as Cinderella had dreamed, she and the Prince were married.

It was a joyous, lovely wedding. As the ceremony ended, the Prince and Cinderella ran down the aisle and out of the church. Bluebirds fluttered behind them, carrying Cinderella's train in their beaks.

As Cinderella ran down the church steps, she again lost one of her slippers. This time, however, she turned back to get it. The King was there, waiting. He slipped it back on her foot. Cinderella planted a kiss on the top of his head and ran back to join her Prince.

All of Cinderella's animal friends had come to the wedding and were there to see her off. Jaq and Gus waved good-bye as she stepped into her carriage. Bruno ran alongside, barking his congratulations. The carriage rolled off. It moved slowly down the road and through a grand stone archway. The Prince and Cinderella kissed.

It was the end of a lovely fairy tale. Once, Cinderella had been scorned and treated cruelly. Now she was a princess. And all because she had held fast to her dreams. Cinderella and her Prince rode off to their new life together. They lived happily ever after.